CERAMIC TILES
VALENTINE
COLOR BY NUMBER

CERAMIC TILES
VALENTINE
COLOR BY NUMBER

Brighten your heart and fill your days with love while coloring these Adorable Ceramic tiles Color By Number pages.

The Valentine themed 25 Ceramic tile designs with easy to follow color by numbers of vibrant 21 colors are here to make your days full of love and perfect to bring you in valentine mood.

These easy to color - color by number designs are simple yet attractive. Beautiful repeatable patterns, mandala styles; are perfect for those who want to spend their time enjoying coloring in the Season of Love.

Book Features:

• Easy to color 8 ½ x 8 ½ inch pages.

• Single-sided, with black back page to minimize the color bleed visibility.

• Color by numbers to follow and complete the page giving you tremendous relaxation and satisfaction.

• Cutting borders for easy cut off pages to gift / display.

• Unique valentine designs on ceramic tiles.

!! Happy coloring !!

By Prachi Dewan Sachdeva

1 Brown 2 Red Brown 3 LT. Brown

4 Red 5 Orange 6 Yellow

7 Dark Green 8 Green 9 LT. Green

10 Blue 11 Turquoise 12 LT. Blue

13 Purple 14 Lavender 15 Magenta

16 Hot Pink 17 Pink 18 Peach

19 Grey 20 Dark Grey 21 Black

1 Brown

2 Red Brown

3 LT. Brown

4 Red

5 Orange

6 Yellow

7 Dark Green

8 Green

9 LT. Green

10 Blue

11 Turquoise

12 LT. Blue

13 Purple

14 Lavender

15 Magenta

16 Hot Pink

17 Pink

18 Peach

19 Grey

20 Dark Grey

21 Black

1 Brown
2 Red Brown
3 LT. Brown
4 Red
5 Orange
6 Yellow
7 Dark Green
8 Green
9 LT. Green
10 Blue
11 Turquoise
12 LT. Blue
13 Purple
14 Lavender
15 Magenta
16 Hot Pink
17 Pink
18 Peach
19 Grey
20 Dark Grey
21 Black

1 Brown   2 Red Brown   3 LT. Brown

4 Red   5 Orange   6 Yellow

7 Dark Green   8 Green   9 LT. Green

10 Blue   11 Turquoise   12 LT. Blue

13 Purple   14 Lavender   15 Magenta

16 Hot Pink   17 Pink   18 Peach

19 Grey   20 Dark Grey   21 Black

1 Brown
2 Red Brown
3 LT. Brown
4 Red
5 Orange
6 Yellow
7 Dark Green
8 Green
9 LT. Green
10 Blue
11 Turquoise
12 LT. Blue
13 Purple
14 Lavender
15 Magenta
16 Hot Pink
17 Pink
18 Peach
19 Grey
20 Dark Grey
21 Black

1 Brown	2 Red Brown	3 LT. Brown
4 Red	5 Orange	6 Yellow
7 Dark Green	8 Green	9 LT. Green
10 Blue	11 Turquoise	12 LT. Blue
13 Purple	14 Lavender	15 Magenta
16 Hot Pink	17 Pink	18 Peach
19 Grey	20 Dark Grey	21 Black

1 Brown	2 Red Brown	3 LT. Brown
4 Red	5 Orange	6 Yellow
7 Dark Green	8 Green	9 LT. Green
10 Blue	11 Turquoise	12 LT. Blue
13 Purple	14 Lavender	15 Magenta
16 Hot Pink	17 Pink	18 Peach
19 Grey	20 Dark Grey	21 Black

1 Brown
2 Red Brown
3 LT. Brown
4 Red
5 Orange
6 Yellow
7 Dark Green
8 Green
9 LT. Green
10 Blue
11 Turquoise
12 LT. Blue
13 Purple
14 Lavender
15 Magenta
16 Hot Pink
17 Pink
18 Peach
19 Grey
20 Dark Grey
21 Black

1 Brown
2 Red Brown
3 LT. Brown
4 Red
5 Orange
6 Yellow
7 Dark Green
8 Green
9 LT. Green
10 Blue
11 Turquoise
12 LT. Blue
13 Purple
14 Lavender
15 Magenta
16 Hot Pink
17 Pink
18 Peach
19 Grey
20 Dark Grey
21 Black

1 Brown
2 Red Brown
3 LT. Brown
4 Red
5 Orange
6 Yellow
7 Dark Green
8 Green
9 LT. Green
10 Blue
11 Turquoise
12 LT. Blue
13 Purple
14 Lavender
15 Magenta
16 Hot Pink
17 Pink
18 Peach
19 Grey
20 Dark Grey
21 Black

1 Brown   2 Red Brown   3 LT. Brown

4 Red   5 Orange   6 Yellow

7 Dark Green   8 Green   9 LT. Green

10 Blue   11 Turquoise   12 LT. Blue

13 Purple   14 Lavender   15 Magenta

16 Hot Pink   17 Pink   18 Peach

19 Grey   20 Dark Grey   21 Black

1 Brown	2 Red Brown	3 LT. Brown
4 Red	5 Orange	6 Yellow
7 Dark Green	8 Green	9 LT. Green
10 Blue	11 Turquoise	12 LT. Blue
13 Purple	14 Lavender	15 Magenta
16 Hot Pink	17 Pink	18 Peach
19 Grey	20 Dark Grey	21 Black

1	Brown	2	Red Brown	3	LT. Brown
4	Red	5	Orange	6	Yellow
7	Dark Green	8	Green	9	LT. Green
10	Blue	11	Turquoise	12	LT. Blue
13	Purple	14	Lavender	15	Magenta
16	Hot Pink	17	Pink	18	Peach
19	Grey	20	Dark Grey	21	Black

1 Brown   2 Red Brown   3 LT. Brown

4 Red   5 Orange   6 Yellow

7 Dark Green   8 Green   9 LT. Green

10 Blue   11 Turquoise   12 LT. Blue

13 Purple   14 Lavender   15 Magenta

16 Hot Pink   17 Pink   18 Peach

19 Grey   20 Dark Grey   21 Black

1 Brown

2 Red Brown

3 LT. Brown

4 Red

5 Orange

6 Yellow

7 Dark Green

8 Green

9 LT. Green

10 Blue

11 Turquoise

12 LT. Blue

13 Purple

14 Lavender

15 Magenta

16 Hot Pink

17 Pink

18 Peach

19 Grey

20 Dark Grey

21 Black

1 Brown   2 Red Brown   3 LT. Brown

4 Red   5 Orange   6 Yellow

7 Dark Green   8 Green   9 LT. Green

10 Blue   11 Turquoise   12 LT. Blue

13 Purple   14 Lavender   15 Magenta

16 Hot Pink   17 Pink   18 Peach

19 Grey   20 Dark Grey   21 Black

1 Brown

2 Red Brown

3 LT. Brown

4 Red

5 Orange

6 Yellow

7 Dark Green

8 Green

9 LT. Green

10 Blue

11 Turquoise

12 LT. Blue

13 Purple

14 Lavender

15 Magenta

16 Hot Pink

17 Pink

18 Peach

19 Grey

20 Dark Grey

21 Black

1 Brown
2 Red Brown
3 LT. Brown
4 Red
5 Orange
6 Yellow
7 Dark Green
8 Green
9 LT. Green
10 Blue
11 Turquoise
12 LT. Blue
13 Purple
14 Lavender
15 Magenta
16 Hot Pink
17 Pink
18 Peach
19 Grey
20 Dark Grey
21 Black

1 Brown   2 Red Brown   3 LT. Brown

4 Red   5 Orange   6 Yellow

7 Dark Green   8 Green   9 LT. Green

10 Blue   11 Turquoise   12 LT. Blue

13 Purple   14 Lavender   15 Magenta

16 Hot Pink   17 Pink   18 Peach

19 Grey   20 Dark Grey   21 Black

1 Brown	2 Red Brown	3 LT. Brown
4 Red	5 Orange	6 Yellow
7 Dark Green	8 Green	9 LT. Green
10 Blue	11 Turquoise	12 LT. Blue
13 Purple	14 Lavender	15 Magenta
16 Hot Pink	17 Pink	18 Peach
19 Grey	20 Dark Grey	21 Black

1 Brown	2 Red Brown	3 LT. Brown
4 Red	5 Orange	6 Yellow
7 Dark Green	8 Green	9 LT. Green
10 Blue	11 Turquoise	12 LT. Blue
13 Purple	14 Lavender	15 Magenta
16 Hot Pink	17 Pink	18 Peach
19 Grey	20 Dark Grey	21 Black

1. Brown
2. Red Brown
3. LT. Brown
4. Red
5. Orange
6. Yellow
7. Dark Green
8. Green
9. LT. Green
10. Blue
11. Turquoise
12. LT. Blue
13. Purple
14. Lavender
15. Magenta
16. Hot Pink
17. Pink
18. Peach
19. Grey
20. Dark Grey
21. Black

1 Brown
2 Red Brown
3 LT. Brown
4 Red
5 Orange
6 Yellow
7 Dark Green
8 Green
9 LT. Green
10 Blue
11 Turquoise
12 LT. Blue
13 Purple
14 Lavender
15 Magenta
16 Hot Pink
17 Pink
18 Peach
19 Grey
20 Dark Grey
21 Black

1 Brown
2 Red Brown
3 LT. Brown
4 Red
5 Orange
6 Yellow
7 Dark Green
8 Green
9 LT. Green
10 Blue
11 Turquoise
12 LT. Blue
13 Purple
14 Lavender
15 Magenta
16 Hot Pink
17 Pink
18 Peach
19 Grey
20 Dark Grey
21 Black

1. Brown
2. Red Brown
3. LT. Brown
4. Red
5. Orange
6. Yellow
7. Dark Green
8. Green
9. LT. Green
10. Blue
11. Turquoise
12. LT. Blue
13. Purple
14. Lavender
15. Magenta
16. Hot Pink
17. Pink
18. Peach
19. Grey
20. Dark Grey
21. Black

COLOR CHART

Medium: _____ Date: _____

1

2

3

4

5

6

7

8

9

10

11

12

13

14

15

16

17

18

19

20

21

COLOR CHART

Medium:_____ Date:_____

1

2

3

4

5

6

7

8

9

10

11

12

13

14

15

16

17

18

19

20

21

COLOR CHART

Medium:_____   Date:_____

1

2

3

4

5

6

7

8

9

10

11

12

13

14

15

16

17

18

19

20

21

COLOR CHART

Medium: _____   Date: _____

1

2

3

4

5

6

7

8

9

10

11

12

13

14

15

16

17

18

19

20

21

If You Enjoyed Coloring These Valentine Ceramic Tiles Please Rate Us On Amazon

Prachi Dewan Sachdeva
(Author & Illustrator)

Made in United States
Orlando, FL
05 January 2023

28217061R00037